For Matthew and Pop

LADYBIRD BOOKS, INC.
Auburn, Maine 04210 U.S.A.
LADYBIRD BOOKS LTD
Loughborough, Leicestershire, England
© EUGENIE FERNANDES 1990

Printed in England

ALONE TOGETHER
a book about opposites

By Eugenie Fernandes

Ladybird Books

The Beginning

Poppa was kind and wise and funny.

Peter loved Poppa. He didn't want to share him with anyone else.

Whenever they were together, Peter would say, "Can we be alone?"

Poppa would smile and nod and say,
"Alone—together!"

Peter was rather **young**.

Poppa was rather **old**.

Poppa was **tall**. Peter was **short**.

Poppa had **big** hands. Peter had **little** hands.

One day Peter and Poppa went for a walk.

Peter **opened** the gate.

Poppa **closed** the gate.

Poppa walked **slowly**. Peter walked **quickly**.

They walked and they walked,
till they came to an apple tree.

Poppa picked two apples.
One apple tasted **sweet**.
The other one tasted **sour**.

They walked and they walked some more,
till they came to the beach.

They took off their shoes and socks
and walked in the sand.

Poppa said, "The sand is very **warm**.
Let's put our feet in the water."

The water felt nice and **cool**.

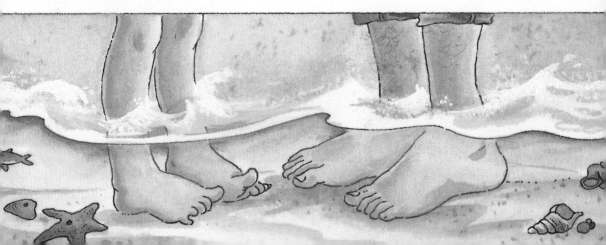

Peter found a feather.
Poppa found a shell.
The feather was **soft**.
The shell was **hard**.

Peter made a castle in the sand.
Carefully, he **built it up**.

Then a wave came and **knocked it down**.

Poppa threw a rock
into the water.
It **sank** to the **bottom**.

Peter threw a stick into the water.
It **floated** on the **top**.

Peter and Poppa lay down on the sand
and looked up at the clouds.

Some of the clouds were **fat**.
Some of the clouds were **thin**.

Some of them were **moving**,
and some of them were **still**.

Soon Poppa fell **asleep**.

Peter stayed **awake**. He watched the birds.

There were **noisy** birds and **quiet** birds…

birds flying **over** the water
and birds diving **under** the water...
all kinds of birds.

After a little while, Poppa woke up.

"Time to go home," he said.

Peter looked **sad**.

"We'll come again tomorrow," said Poppa.

Then Peter looked **happy**.

"Can we be alone tomorrow?" asked Peter.
Poppa smiled and nodded and said,
"Alone—together!"

The End

tall · short

over · under

fat · thin

sweet · sour

fast · slow